This Walker book belongs to:

_____

Sam Hargreaves   20/06/13.

_____

For Danny

First published 1999 by Walker Books Ltd
87 Vauxhall Walk, London SE11 5HJ

This edition published 2001

2 4 6 8 10 9 7 5 3

© 1999 Anita Jeram

This book has been typeset in Kabel-Book Alt

Printed in China

Anita Jeram has asserted her moral rights

British Library Cataloguing in Publication Data:
a catalogue record for this book is
available from the British Library

ISBN 978-0-7445-7857-7

www.walker.co.uk

All Together Now

Anita Jeram

WALKER BOOKS
AND SUBSIDIARIES
LONDON · BOSTON · SYDNEY

When Mummy Rabbit says,
"All together now",
one thing Bunny, Little Duckling
and Miss Mouse often do is sing
their special little Honeys' song.

"All together now!" …

We're the little Honeys.
A little Honey is sweet.
Quack quack, squeak squeak,
Thump your great big feet!

In the little Honeys' song,

"A little Honey is sweet" is Bunny's special line.

Bunny was Mummy Rabbit's first little Honey,

before Little Duckling and Miss Mouse came along.

He was always as sweet as can be.
That's why Mummy Rabbit called him
"Bunny, my Honey".

In the little Honeys' song, "Quack quack"

is Little Duckling's special line.

Its special meaning is,

I'm yellow and fluffy and

good at splashing and sploshing.

It means, even if I don't look like a bunny,

Mummy Rabbit's still my mummy just the same.

When he was born,

Little Duckling came from an egg.

The first surprise was when he hatched out.

Bunny was just peeping at the egg

when it cracked open and out

came Little Duckling.

The next surprise was when
Little Duckling followed Bunny home
and became his brother and
the second little Honey.

In the little Honeys' song, "squeak squeak"

is Miss Mouse's special line.

Its special meaning is,

I've got a pink itchy-titchy nose

and a pink squirly-whirly tail.

It means, even if I don't look like a bunny,

Mummy Rabbit's still my mummy just the same.

Miss Mouse first arrived when Bunny
and Little Duckling found her all alone in the
long grass early one summer morning.
Miss Mouse wasn't frightened.
She just seemed to need some
love and affection.

Mummy Rabbit soon made
her one of the family;
a new sister and a third little Honey.

As well as singing their special song,

the little Honeys play all sorts

of special games together.

They play splashy-sploshy games,

which Little Duckling

is best at.

They play itchy-titchy

squirly-whirly games,

which Miss Mouse

is best at.

They play run-rabbit-run games,

which Bunny is best at.

Best of all they play the
Thump-Your-Great-Big-Feet game,
which they are all best at together
because they all have

Great Big Feet.

Bunny has

Great Big Feet.

Little Duckling has
Great **Big** Feet.

Miss Mouse has
Great **Big** Feet.

And sometimes

Mummy Rabbit

plays with them,

which is extra-specially special

because Mummy Rabbit has the

Greatest

Biggest

Feet of all!

The Thump-Your-Great-Big-Feet game goes like this:

thump!

thump!

thump!

thump!

thump!

We're the little Honeys.
A little Honey is sweet.
Quack quack, squeak squeak,
Thump Your Great Big Feet!

Another Little Honeys story

Bunny My Honey

Anita Jeram

ISBN 978-0-7445-7283-4

Available from all good booksellers

www.walker.co.uk